BAD  KITTY

MAKES COMICS . . .

AND YOU CAN TOO!

NICK BRUEL

SQUARE
FISH

A NEAL PORTER BOOK
NEW YORK

DEDICATED TO MY FRIEND AND HERO,
THE COMIC MASTER,
JULES FEIFFER

SQUARE
FISH

An Imprint of Macmillan
175 Fifth Avenue
New York, NY 10010

Square Fish and the Square Fish logo are trademarks of Macmillan and
are used by Roaring Brook Press under license from Macmillan.

Square Fish books may be purchased for business or promotional use. For information
on bulk purchases, please contact the Macmillan Corporate and Premium Sales Department at
(800) 221-7945 x5442 or by e-mail at specialmarkets@macmillan.com.

First Square Fish Edition: 2015
Book designed by Kristie Radwilowicz and Jennifer Browne
Square Fish logo designed by Filomena Tuosto

ISBN 978-1-59643-979-5

1 3 5 7 9 10 8 6 4 2

• CONTENTS •

• AN IMPORTANT MESSAGE •

All of the pages in this book are sized to fit on common printer or photocopier paper.

The author of this book invites you to photocopy the exercise pages as much as you'd like so that you can do these exercises as often as you'd like and not muck up your book.

In fact, if the copy you are holding happens to be a library book, then you **ABSOLUTELY MUST, MUST, MUST** photocopy the exercises in this book so that you're not damaging a book that's not yours.

And if you are reading this book digitally, then you **SUPER DUPER, ABSOLUTELY, UNCONDITIONALLY MUST, MUST, MUST, MUST, MUST*** print out the exercise pages.

Well, you could draw on the computer screen if you wanted to . . . but that's been known to upset some people.

*MUST, MUST, MUST, MUST

• PREFACE •

When I was in third grade, not only did I READ comic books, but I also MADE comic books.

My friends Jimmy, Paul, Deirdre, and I formed our own comic book company. Sometimes I would write a story, and Jimmy would illustrate it. Sometimes Deirdre would write a story, and Paul would illustrate it. And sometimes we would switch roles so that Deirdre and I could illustrate. We all had these great ideas that we wanted to see made real on paper.

I remember these days so clearly. After spending every free moment we could find making comics in school, we would meet up at each other's houses to keep working on them. Sometimes we were able to make an entire comic book in a single day. Sometimes it took us weeks. It was hard work. But it was always fun.

The Bad Kitty books would not exist today if not for those comics I made back in third grade. Those were the days when I first figured out how to write a story and make drawings to go along with them. My stories and my drawings were very clumsy at first. But I kept trying and I kept getting better.

And now I write and draw stories for a living. I write and draw stories every day. And I love my work now as much as I loved my work back in third grade.

I want EVERYONE to write and draw stories. That's why I made this book. I want every kid in the world to try his or her hand at making comics. It's the best way I know of in which a kid can learn to both write and draw a story at the same time.

So, let's get started. Hopefully, by the time you finish reading this book, you'll have all the knowledge you need to make your own comics all by yourself. And when you do begin writing and illustrating your own stories, I can guarantee only two things: it will be hard work, but it will also be FUN!

• INTRODUCTION •

The sun was not sunny.
The skies were all gray.
Kitty sat in her home
Through that cold, wet, gray day.

She was so bored
As she sat on her butt
She thought that she might
Even play with the mutt.

But that would be crazy!
She'd rather be sick.

She decided a nap
Just might do the trick.

And that's just what she did.

Sleep!
    Sleep!
        Sleep!
            Sleep!

She counted her sheep
Until her sleep, it was deep.

And then something went **KNOCK!**

That knock was a shock!

Then it happened again
and again!
Oh, what a block of
knock shocks!

KNOCK
KNOCK
KNOCK
KNOCK

That's when she saw him,
Wet as a rat.
That's when she saw . . .

A cat in a hat.

And he said to Kitty,
"I know things are dull,
But I've got some fun
to jam in your skull!"

"I have the cure!
In my bag are the tonics!
We'll spend this wet day . . .

MAKING SOME

COMICS!"

"I have paper and pencils
And brushes and ink!
I have rulers and even
Some markers, I think!"

You see, there are hundreds of magazines in the United States alone that publish cartoons. There are over 6,000 daily newspapers in the world today, and thousands more that are weekly or monthly, and nearly all of them have comic strips. And literally **MILLIONS** of comic books are sold every month.

But you're not interested. Sooooo . . .Toodles!

"I KNOW JUST WHAT I'LL DO!"
Said the cat with a yelp.
"I'll go into my bag
Where I keep some help."

"There are things in this bag
That do not have fleas!
There are things in this bag
That like to eat cheese!"

"There are things in this bag
That like to have FUN!
I call the things in this bag . . ."

34

· EXERCISE ·

Different tools can have different results. Below are six different drawings of Kitty using six different drawing tools.

Pencil

Ball point pen

Marker

Crayon

Brush and Ink

Computer

Now it's YOUR turn! First, I want you to find as many drawing tools as you can find. Take your time. I'll wait. Now I want you to draw a **circle** with each of those tools. You can do this below or on a fresh piece of paper.

Which tool do you like the most? Which one do you like least?

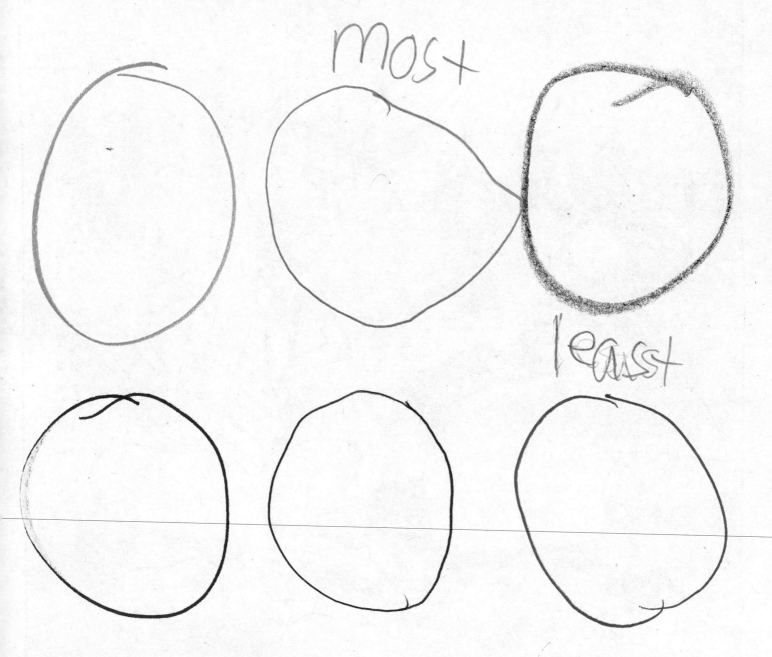

most

least

40

A **CARTOON**, or "single panel comic," has just ONE panel.

"I WISH I HAD AN OCTOPUS!"

(Words that are placed underneath a panel are called a "caption.")

A **COMIC STRIP** can have just one or lots of panels, but they all fit next to each other in a single row or column.

I WISH I HAD AN OCTOPUS!

HEY! I'M AN OCTOPUS!

I'M SO HAPPY!

A COMIC BOOK has lots of pages, and each page can have lots of panels.

Let's practice making some panels on a comic page. Below are some examples of how you can fit four panels onto a single page.

Now it's YOUR turn! How would you go about fitting five or six or more panels onto a single page?

You can try your hand in the pages below or on separate sheets of paper.

© Nick Bruel

· EXERCISE ·

In comics, the words you write and the story you tell are just as important as the drawings. I've drawn some dots here. Now I'm going to pretend they're ants. The captions underneath each panel will tell their story.

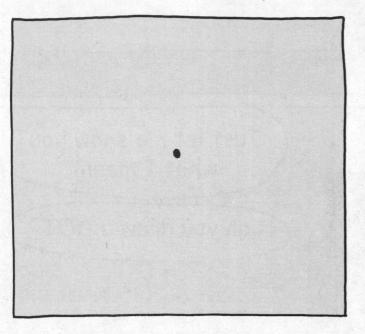

One ant standing by itself in the snow.

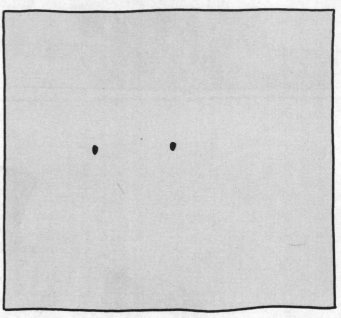

Two ants lying on their back looking up at the clouds.

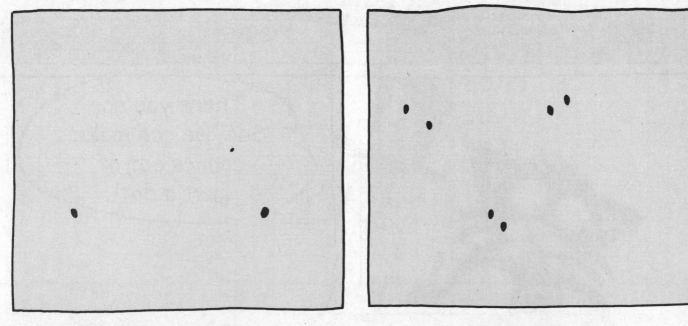

Two ants playing catch.

Six ants dancing.

Now it's YOUR turn!

Write captions underneath each of these panels to tell the story of these ants. After you're done, try it again! See how many stories you can find for these ants.

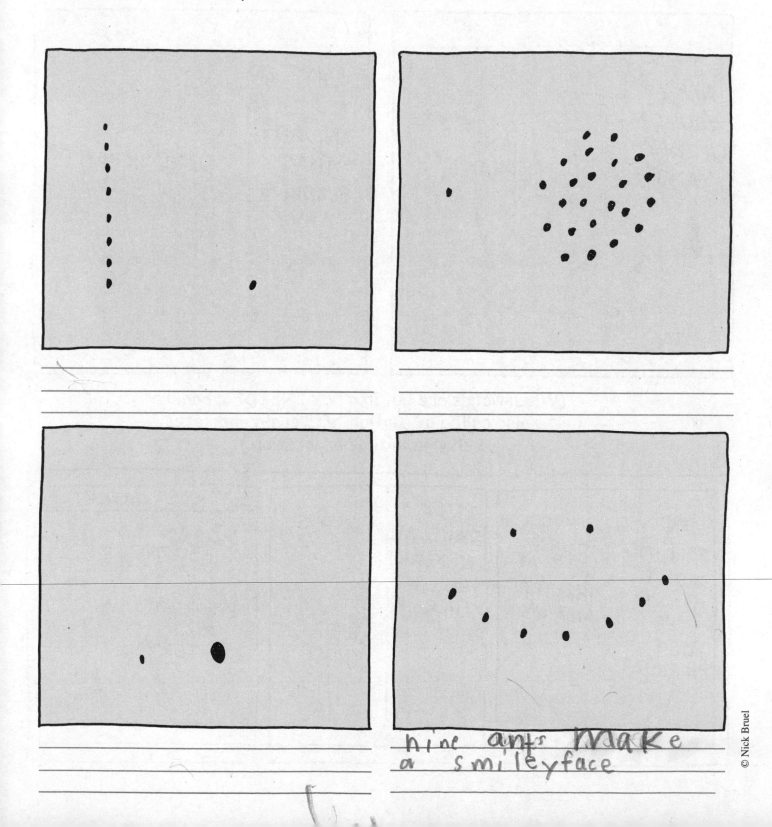

hine ants make
a smileyface

Great! Now let's put some words INSIDE the panels so the ants can talk to each other. When characters talk to each other in a story, that's called "dialogue."

WHAT DO YOU CALL A BABY ANT?

AN INF-ANT!

WHAT DO YOU GIVE AN ANT THAT SMELLS BAD?

DEODOR-ANT!

(When words are put in a box INSIDE a panel, it's also called a "caption." It usually indicates a change in time or location.)

CAN YOU TELL ME HOW TO GET TO THE POST OFFICE?

TURN LEFT AT THE TREE AND WALK 5 MILES.

IT'LL TAKE ME 10 YEARS TO GET THERE!

GOOD LUCK!

3 YEARS LATER...

BACK SO SOON?

I FORGOT MY LETTER!

You know what to do!

Give these ants some dialogue. Maybe these ants like each other. Maybe not. Maybe they're complete strangers. Maybe the ants are funny. Or maybe they're frightened. It's all up to you. And just like on the other page, you can do this again and again when you're done.

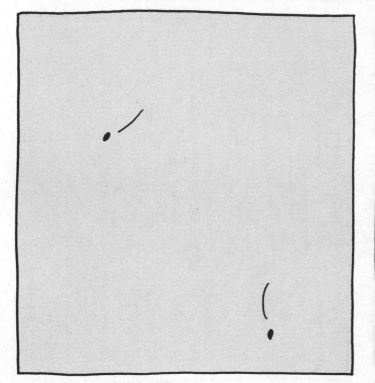
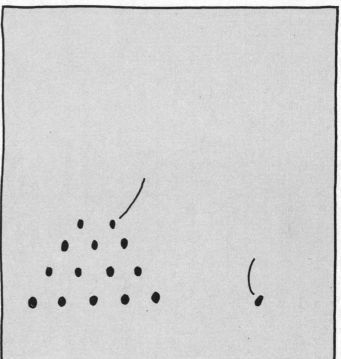

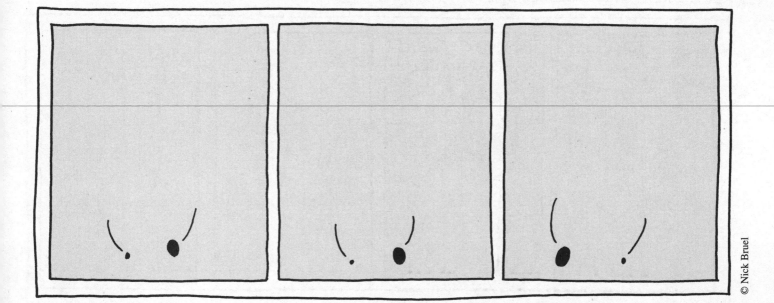

© Nick Bruel

(That line that goes across the panel is called a "horizon line."
It gives the illusion of distance.
Any drawing that has a background will have a horizon line.)

 Your turn! Write some captions and/or dialogue for these dot comics!

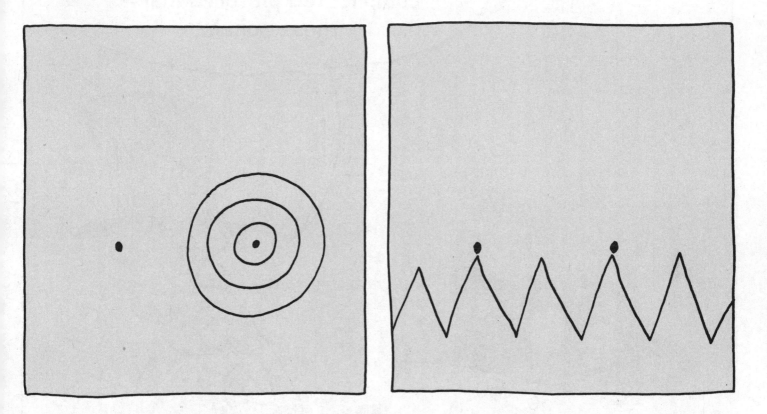

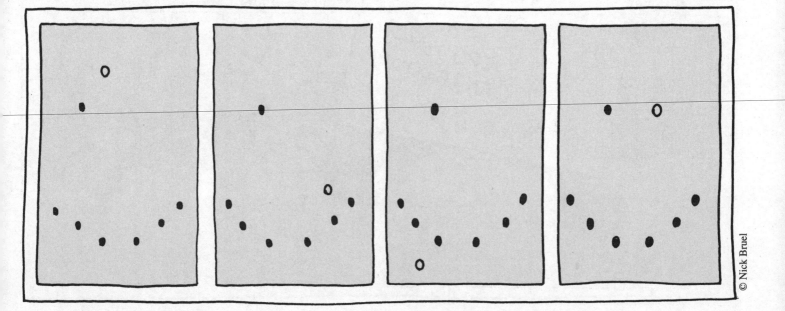

Everytime you combine and move around these shapes, you get something. For instance, you can make a house . . .

. . . or a scooter . . .   . . . or a watermelon sandwich.

Now let's take some shapes and add some dots and some lines to make faces. Not so hard, right?

But we don't need just ROUND shapes to make faces.

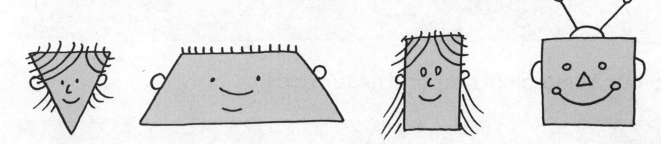

Cool. Now let's make some faces with some REALLY unusual shapes. You can put a face on pretty much any shape out there. In fact, I DARE you to find a shape on which I couldn't put a face.

Hmmm . . . All of these faces are smiling. We can't have that. We need expressions! We need EMOTIONS! Emotions make the characters in our comics seem real.

Let's put some emotions on these faces!

Surprised

Serious

Sad

Scared

Puzzled

Angry

Overjoyed

In Love

66

· EXERCISE ·

You guessed it! YOUR TURN! Using the faces on the opposite page as models, try giving these empty shapes some emotion.

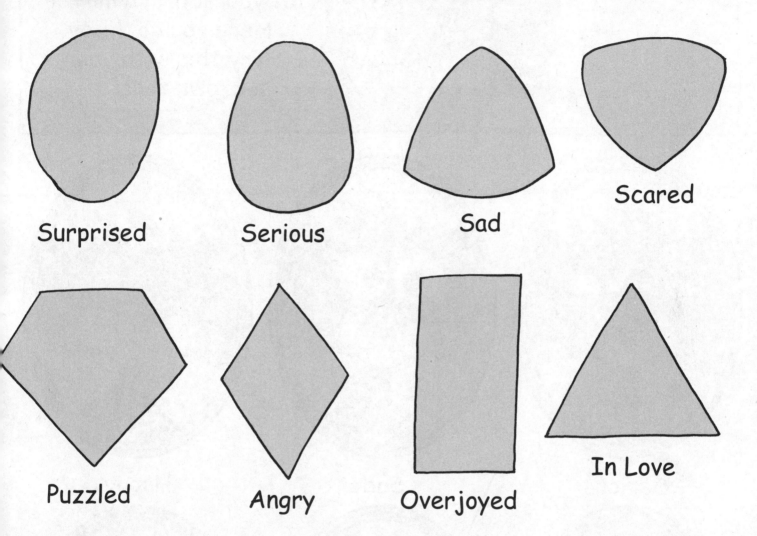

Surprised

Serious

Sad

Scared

Puzzled

Angry

Overjoyed

In Love

Ready for a challenge? Now try putting some emotions we nave NOT reviewed on to these shapes!

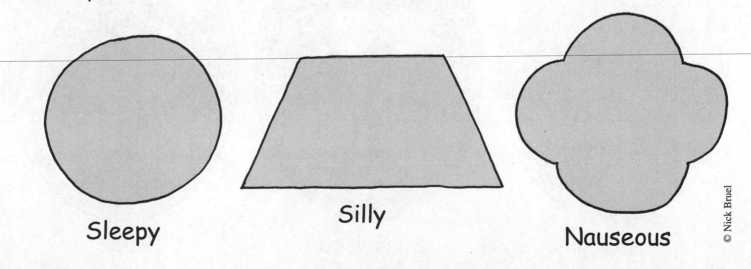

Sleepy

Silly

Nauseous

One great way to learn how to draw facial expressions is to look at yourself in a mirror. Here you go, Kitty. Try this with your own face!

Serious

Sad

Happy

Angry

Surprised

Rude

· EXERCISE ·

Things are starting to get a little complex now! Below are some outlines of Kitty's face. Try drawing her expressions yourself based on what you saw on the last few pages.

Serious

Surprised

Rude

Puzzled

Overjoyed

In Love

Now try your hand at making some expressions for Kitty that we have NOT reviewed. If you need any help, try making faces in the mirror. (You might want to do this when no one else is looking. People don't always understand the creative process.)

Sleepy

Silly

Nauseous

· EXERCISE ·

Let's try using ALL of these different word balloons. I'll go first, then YOU write your own dialogue into the empty balloons!

Now try making your own word balloons, too!

· EXERCISE ·

Let's experiment! I'm going to tell a story, then I want you to use pictures instead of words to have Kitty tell the same story.

AS I WAS WALKING DOWN THE STREET...

I SAW AN OCTOPUS ON A SKATEBOARD SINGING OLD SHOW TUNES.

IT WAS DELICIOUS.

 Now try filling in these balloons with pictures instead of words to tell the story below starring Kitty and Puppy.

Sound effects can be loads of fun. They can take on all sorts of shapes and sizes.

· EXERCISE ·

Take each sound effect and draw how you think it should look!

POW!

ZAP!

EEK!

SPLASH!

Sound effects don't always have to make sense. It can be funny if you take items that you recognize and give them sounds that aren't obvious.

Now let's take these same common items and give them sounds you might not expect.

All of a sudden, these items have become a lot more interesting! And all we did was change the sounds they make.

· EXERCISE ·

Create sound effects for each of these events. Be creative!

A car
exploding

An alien
spaceship
landing

A baby
biting
a clown's
finger

A piano
falling out
a window
and
landing
in wet
cement.

Let's do something different! You go about your business, Kitty, and we'll add sound effects to the common events in your day.

You see, Kitty? I've taken away the flies and added flowers to those squiggly lines. Now you smell nice!

Here's a lightbulb! Now it looks like you're having a great idea! Note how those little lines make the lightbulb look like it's glowing.

If I make those drops fly off of you instead of drip off of you, now you look sweaty or worried.

Look angry, Kitty. GOOD! Now I'm going to make those squiggly lines make you look like you're fuming!

Now say something TERRIBLE, Kitty.

We can replace any rude words with random comic symbols and not get into any trouble . . . usually.

· **EXERCISE** ·

A circle all by itself is just a circle sitting there. Add some comic effects to turn the circles into a ball in ACTION!

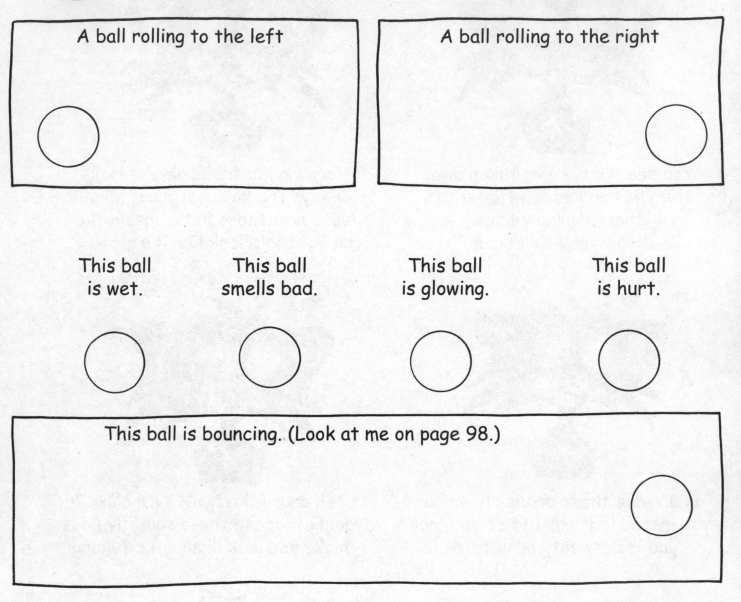

A ball rolling to the left

A ball rolling to the right

This ball
is wet.

This ball
smells bad.

This ball
is glowing.

This ball
is hurt.

This ball is bouncing. (Look at me on page 98.)

Here are a few comic effects we haven't covered.
Let's see what kinds of ideas you can come up with.

This ball
is on fire.

This ball
is underwater.

This ball
is very dusty.

Let's start off slow, Kitty, with some one panel cartoons. What kind of one-panel cartoons can you make about yourself?

"KITTY SAID SHE WAS HUNGRY ENOUGH TO 'EAT A HORSE,' SO..."

KITTY, HAVE YOU SEEN PUPPY?

ARF?

SHIP TO PERU

THIS END UP

KITTY'S GUIDE TO GOOD HEALTH

GET 7 HOURS OF SLEEP EACH NIGHT. THEN ADD AN ADDITIONAL 16.

I'M NOT SURE HOW OR WHY, BUT I THINK KITTY HAS A SUBMARINE.

Your turn! Make some one-panel cartoons about Kitty or ANY character you want. To make things easier, I'm going to start you off with some ideas.

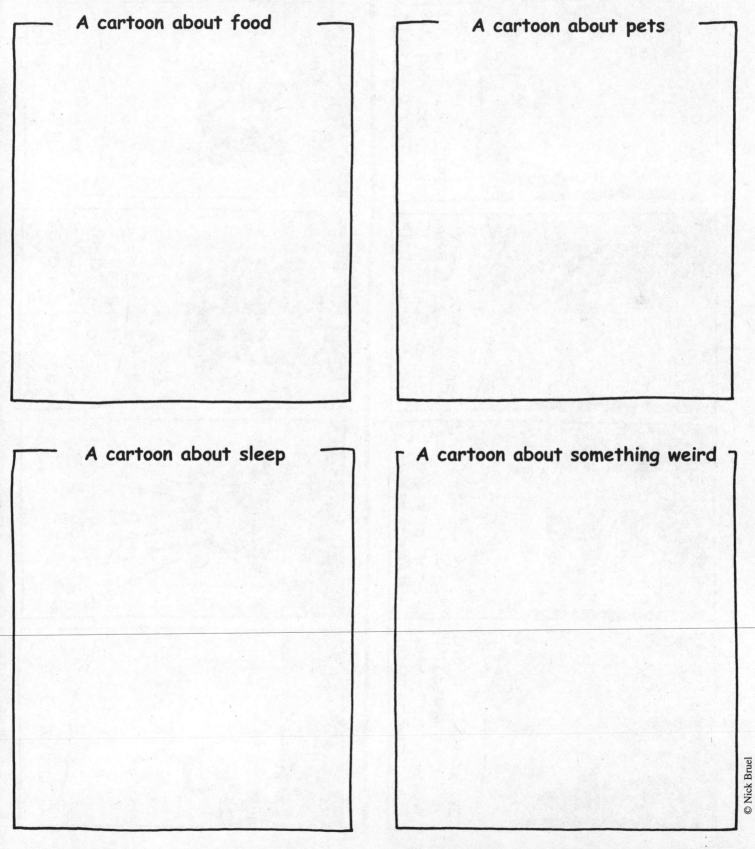

A cartoon about food

A cartoon about pets

A cartoon about sleep

A cartoon about something weird

Now let's make some comic STRIPS about you, Kitty. We're using more panels, so now we can tell a story that's more complicated. To give you more room, I'm turning the page on its side.

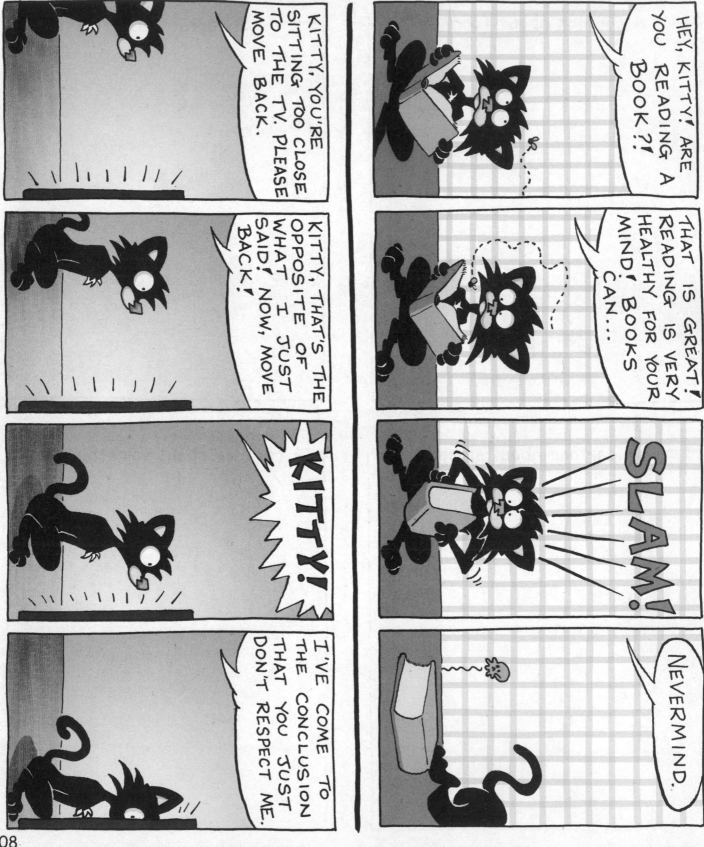

 You know what to do! Try to come up with some comics that need more than one panel to tell the story. I'm giving you ideas again to help you out.

A comic strip about television

A comic strip about books

Comic books are stories that need MANY panels and MANY pages to really do the story any justice.

This time we'll need more than just a character like you, Kitty, to tell the story. Now we'll need something called "CONFLICT." All stories need conflict.

NOT SO FAST!

Here's what we're going to do. Kitty is going to start each two-page adventure. She'll write and illustrate the first page . . .

. . . and then you, dear Reader, are going to finish each adventure. You will write and illustrate the second page below. Use as many or as few panels as you want.

NEW FOOD — STARRING BAD KITTY

Don't just use this page. Get some more sheets of paper and add as many pages as you want to your story.

DOGSITTER — STARRING BAD KITTY

Don't forget to use sound effects!

Try bringing in other characters to make your story even more interesting.

TOYS — STARRING BAD KITTY

 Psst! If you want to make Kitty talk, go ahead. It's YOUR story.

And so the cat thought,
"A job very well done.
We used paper and pencils
And had lots of fun."

The place looked quite messy.
But that was okay.
It's hard to be neat
On a creative day.

He picked up his bag,
And he picked up his mouse
As he opened the door
To exit the house.

The day was not rainy!
Not anymore.
It had stopped raining
Over an hour before.

Should he tell Kitty
That the day was now dry?
No. Let Kitty work.
He won't even say, "Bye."

"But what will YOU do
Now that you've finished this book?
Will you just sit there
And look like a schnook?"

131

"Or will you get busy
Will you draw?
       Will you write?"

"Will you use that big brain
Full of awe and delight?"

"I think that you know,
You know what to do.
The answer is simple.
The answer is true."

• ADVANCED EXERCISES •

HEY, YOU!

Want to earn some extra credit? Sure, you do!

The next several pages are advanced exercises you can do to learn EVEN MORE about making your own comics.

· PANELS ·

The panels we made in Chapter Two: Let's Begin were all rectangular. How many ways can you make a comic page full of panels where NONE of them are rectangles? Get some paper and try it out. Below are some examples. Can you think of any advantages to having non-rectangular panels?

· COMICS WITHOUT DRAWINGS·

In Chapter Three: The Secret to Drawing Comics, we discuss that you don't need to know how to draw to make comics. Instead of drawing a comic, you can always make a COLLAGE COMIC! Take pictures you cut out of a magazine or family pictures you print out from your computer and make a comic out of them. As examples, here are comics made from pictures cut from old magazines and one from a photograph of the author as a child.

· WORD BALLOONS ·

Instead of putting a word into a balloon, what if your word IS the balloon. The result is an interesting combination of word balloons and sound effects. Below are some examples.

Now try making some of your own. Try making "LOOK OUT!" and "HEY!" and "HMMMMMM . . ." and "GOSH!" or anything else you can think of that people sometimes shout out loud.

· SOUND EFFECTS ·

Here's a fun one. Try to come up with a different sound effect for each letter of the alphabet. This is not as easy as it sounds. The trick is to be as creative as you can for some of those lesser used letters like "V" and "Q" and "X."

A _____

B _____

C _____

D _____

E _____

F _____

G _____

H _____

I _____

J _____

K _____

L _____

M _____

N _____

O _____

P _____

Q _____

R _____

S _____

T _____

U _____

V _____

W _____

X _____

Y _____

Z _____

· PUTTING IT ALL TOGETHER ·
(ANOTHER WAY)

Finding a story to tell is not as hard as it sounds. There are literally BILLIONS of stories out there waiting to be told. We call them PEOPLE. Each person alive has a unique story about his or her own life that wants to be heard. All you have to do is have a conversation with that person or ask a few questions in an interview. In fact, the story might even be YOUR OWN!

As an example, below is a comic based on a conversation the author of this book once had with his own daughter.

142

More BAD  KITTY Madness!

NICK BRUEL

BAD KITTY Gets a BATH

The *New York Times* Bestselling Series

NICK BRUEL

BAD KITTY Happy Birthday, BAD KITTY

The *New York Times* Bestselling Series

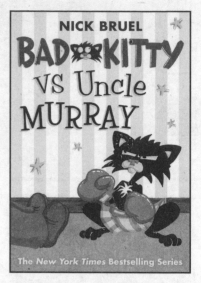

NICK BRUEL

BAD KITTY VS Uncle MURRAY

The *New York Times* Bestselling Series

NICK BRUEL

BAD KITTY Meets the BABY

The *New York Times* Bestselling Series

NICK BRUEL

BAD KITTY for PRESIDENT

The *New York Times* Bestselling Series

NICK BRUEL

BAD KITTY SCHOOL DAZE

The *New York Times* Bestselling Series

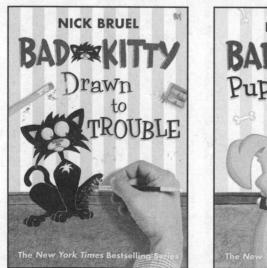

NICK BRUEL

BAD KITTY Drawn to TROUBLE

The *New York Times* Bestselling Series

NICK BRUEL

BAD KITTY Puppy's BIG DAY

The *New York Times* Bestselling Series